For my father, Robbie Jennings, who works for peace – *PG*

For Leah, Ellis & Jodie – *CP*

First published in Great Britain in 2003 by Bloomsbury Publishing Plc
38 Soho Square, London, W1D 3HB

Text copyright © Pippa Goodhart 2003
Illustrations copyright © Colin Paine 2003
The moral right of the author and illustrator has been asserted

A CIP catalogue record of this book is available from the British Library
ISBN 0 7475 5046 8

Designed by Sarah Hodder
Printed in Hong Kong/China by Wing King Tong
Printed in Hong Kong/China by South China Printing Co
Printed in Singapore by Tien Wah Press
1 3 5 7 9 10 8 6 4 2

Arthur's Tractor

by Pippa Goodhart
illustrated by Colin Paine

BLOOMSBURY
CHILDREN'S
BOOKS

Arthur's tractor ploughed up and down, turning green to brown.

Chugga thrum, chugga thrum, chugga chugga thrum.

Chugga thrum, chugga thrum, chugga chugga –

EEEK!

Arthur stamped down the brake and stopped the tractor.
'Well, knobble my kneecaps, whatever can that EEEK be?'

Arthur turned off the engine and got down from his cab. He stood for a while and scratched his head, then he said, 'That must be the sprocket spring sprigget needs a twist and an oil.'

So Arthur twisted and oiled.

He started up his tractor, and now
there was no EEEK, just ...

Chugga thrum, chugga thrum,

chugga chugga thrum.

'Good,' said Arthur.

Chugga thrum, chugga thrum, chugga chugga

THUD THUD THUD!

'Well, bless my blisters, whatever can that be?' Arthur turned off the engine and got down from his cab. He stood for a while and scratched his head, then he said,

THUD THUD THUD

'That must be the old bundle weaver running loose.'
So he gave the bundle weaver a kick, and when he started up
his tractor there was no THUD THUD THUD, just ...

Chugga thrum, chugga thrum, chugga chugga thrum

'Good,' said Arthur. Then …

Chugga thrum, chugga thrum, chugga chugga

CRASH!

'Well, top and tail a turnip, whatever can that CRASH be?' Arthur turned off the engine and got down from his cab. He stood for a while and he scratched his head, then he said, 'That must have been the curling blade hitting a stone. That'll have to be sheared and shuffled and sharpened now.'

So Arthur took out his tools.

He sheared.

He shuffled.

He began to sharpen …
but something jogged his arm
and the curling blade shattered.

'Oh dollops of dung, the blim blam blade has broken!'

'Here,' said Arthur.
'Might I have that old sword?'

'And if you could blow there,
that'd help.'

'Might I have a bit of that to wipe the blade clean?'

'And if you'd hold that in place that'd help.'

Arthur and his new
friend Edith hemmed
and jiggered and
fixed a fine sharp
new curling blade.

The blade was fixed, but the lady lingered.

'That's a finely tuned and turned out tractor you've got there,' she said.

'It is,' said Arthur. 'But, if I might say so, Edith, you're rather well tuned and turned out yourself.'

'Oh!' said Lady Edith. 'And you, Arthur, are as handsome as a well polished tractor bonnet.'

'Nobody's ever said the like of that to me before,' said Arthur.

Arthur took off his cap and he scratched his head
and he thought for a while, then he said, 'Would you
care to share this tractor with me, Edith? And the
soil too? We could sow and reap together and for ever.
What do you say?'

'I say, that'd be good,' said Lady Edith. 'Now pass me
that can and I'll oil that coil bolt brandisher before
the dang thing bangles free.'

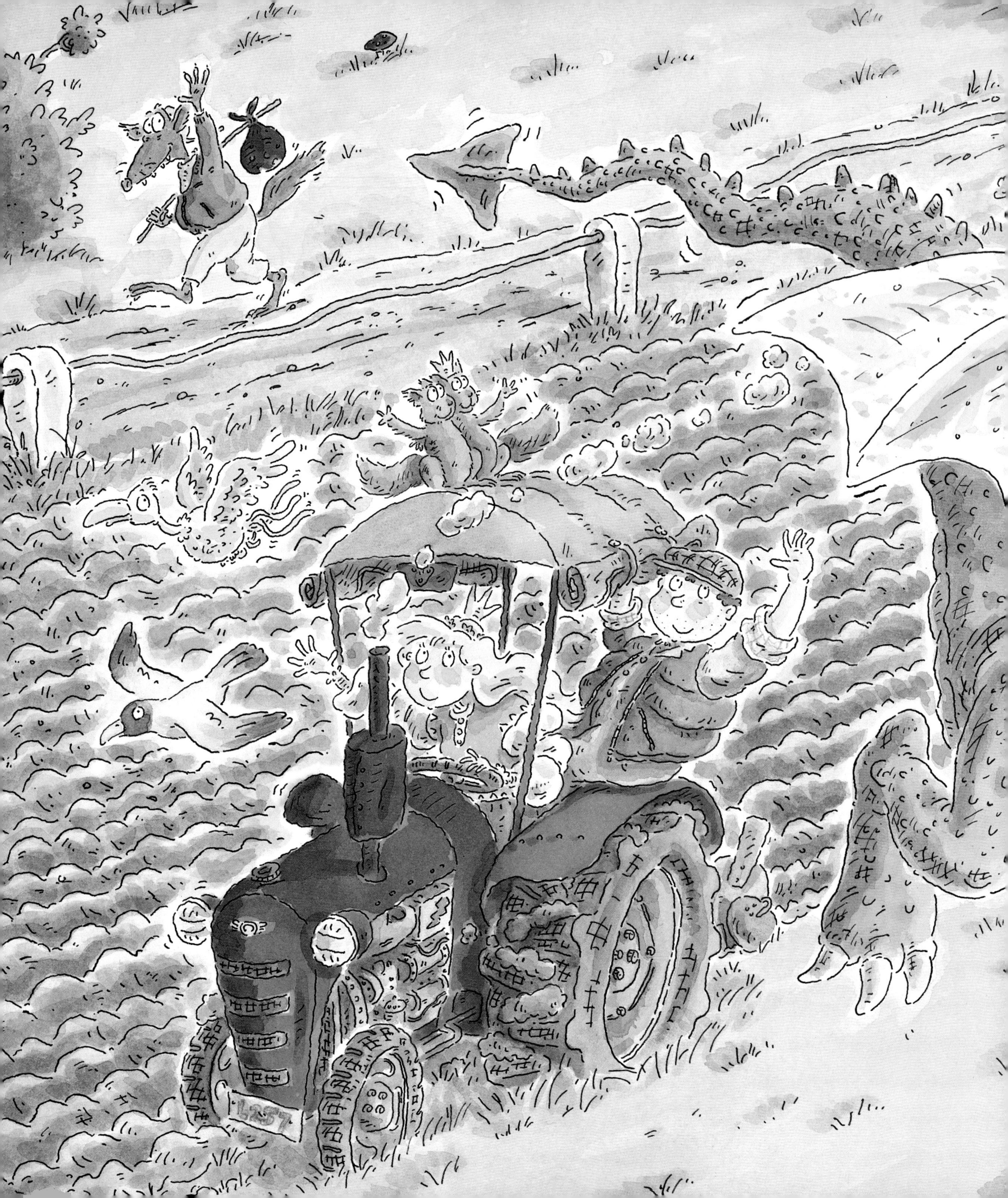

And they all lived happily ever after.